Joseph Towers

A Letter to the Right Honourable the Earl of Shelburne

First Lord of the Treasury

Joseph Towers

A Letter to the Right Honourable the Earl of Shelburne
First Lord of the Treasury

ISBN/EAN: 9783337195694

Printed in Europe, USA, Canada, Australia, Japan

Cover: Foto ©Andreas Hilbeck / pixelio.de

More available books at **www.hansebooks.com**

A

LETTER

T O

THE RIGHT HONOURABLE

THE EARL OF SHELBURNE.

[PRICE ONE SHILLING.]

A

LETTER

TO

THE RIGHT HONOURABLE

THE EARL OF SHELBURNE,

FIRST LORD OF THE TREASURY.

ILLE DOLIS INSTRUCTUS ET ARTE PELASGA.
VIRGIL.

LONDON:
PRINTED FOR CHARLES DILLY, IN THE POULTRY.
MDCCLXXXII.

A LETTER

TO

THE RIGHT HONOURABLE

THE EARL OF SHELBURNE.

My Lord,

AT a time when the affairs of this country were in the higheſt degree critical, when the nation had been brought almoſt to the brink of ruin by an adminiſtration, whoſe conduct had rendered them the juſt objects of public execration, and of public puniſhment, your lordſhip was called to take a ſhare in the councils of your ſovereign, and placed in an elevated and

B   important

important ftation. Other noblemen and gentlemen, diftinguifhed for their abilities, and their fteady oppofition to 'the meafures of the late miniftry, were called into office at the fame time; and from your united efforts confiderable expectations were formed, that the national calamities might at leaft be in fome degree alleviated, that a plan of public œconomy might be adopted, and that fome ftop might be put to a war, which had been commenced in wickednefs and in folly, which had been carried on with the moft wanton profufion of blood and of treafure, and by which Great Britain had been injured and difgraced beyond the example of any former period.

BUT though men flattered themfelves, when your lordfhip came into office, that you would co-operate with others

in

in promoting the interests of the nation,
yet it was not in the Earl of Shelburne
that the public chiefly reposed their confidence. In the speeches of your lordship in parliament, in oppofition to the
meafures of the late adminiftration, you
had manifefted a juft fenfe of the dangerous fituation into which the nation
had been brought by the American
war, and of the neceffity of public œconomy; you had pointed out, in very
energetic language, the pernicious ten-
dency of the influence of the crown ;
and you had difplayed a confiderable
knowledge of the political connexions,
interefts, and tranfactions of foreign na-
tions. But though you had thereby
rendered yourfelf confpicuous in the
houfe of peers, yet, from whatever caufe
it proceeded, the public appear not to
have had that confidence in the rectitude of your intentions, and the up-

rightnefs

rightnefs of your views, which they had in fome others who engaged in the oppofition. Your conduct, fince your entrance into power, has unhappily afforded too much evidence, that the fufpicion and diftruft of your lordfhip which had been entertained, were not without foundation.

THE removal of the laft iniquitous and moft corrupt miniftry, and the appointment of men in their ftead who profeffed principles totally oppofite, and who had avowed an ardent attachment to the rights and liberties of the people, was a moft important political revolution. It was an event which the fpirit of the nation ought long before to have effected, but which a concurrence of circumftances at length brought about, when there feemed little reafon to form any fuch expectation. It was, however,

very

very early feen, that the ftability of the
new miniftry depended upon their union;
and fome apprehenfions were formed of
differences among them, on account of
a known diverfity of fentiment on cer-
tain points. But it was hoped, that a
regard to their common intereft, and to
the welfare of the nation, which could
not be effentially promoted but by their
unanimity, would prevent their having
any fuch open difagreements, as would
be injurious to the public fervice. Nor
was it expected, that the ambition of an
individual, who was defirous of obtaining an afcendancy in the cabinet, would
have deftroyed the faireft hopes that had
been formed of important national be-
nefits from the new adminiftration.

THE death of the late Marquis of
ROCKINGHAM, an event greatly to be
lamented by the real friends to the beft
interefts

interefts of this country, gave an opportunity to your lordfhip to aim at obtaining a more elevated ftation ; and of
convincing every intelligent obferver,
that your own aggrandizement was much
more the objeƈt of your attention, than
the welfare of your country ; or than
that union in the cabinet, among men
of truly public principles, which could
only effeƈtuate the falvation of the nation, at a period of fo much calamity
and danger. Without the approbation
of your colleagues in office, you haftily
and privately obtained from his majefty
a grant of the office of firft lord of the
treafury ; without appearing to give
yourfelf much concern, whether this
was an appointment agreeable to thofe
with whom you had hitherto aƈted, or
whether they would continue to aƈt
under the arrangement which would be
the refult of your lordfhip's elevation.

This

This was a ftep naturally calculated to deftroy that union, without which the great interefts of the people could not be promoted, and which therefore it cannot be fuppofed that your lordfhip would have taken, if you had been actuated by a fincere attachment to the welfare of the nation, or if your own perfonal aggrandizement had not been the ultimate object of your aim.

It is pretended by your friends, that you had a juft and reafonable claim to the office you now hold, upon the death of the late Marquis of Rockingham, from your rank, abilities, and influence. Admitting this to be your opinion, it might be very natural for you, when that unfortunate event happened, to ftate your pretenfions to the other noblemen and gentlemen, who were affociated with your lordfhip in the

the new adminiftration. But if you had really been influenced by a regard to the interefts of the public, you would certainly have continued in the ftation in which you were, when you found your removal to the treafury difagreeable to your colleagues, rather than the nation fhould have loft the fervices of Mr. Fox and Mr. BURKE, men who each of them poffeffed abilities much fuperior to your own; or rather than have been the means of breaking up an adminiftration, from which the public had formed fuch flattering expectations.

BUT it has been intimated, by your lordfhip and your friends, that if his majefty thought proper to place you at the head of the treafury, he had an undoubted right to do it by virtue of his royal prerogative, nor had the reft of his minifters any right to oppofe it.

2   With

With refpect to his majefty's prerogative, that will enable him at any time to
make a peer of the weakeft, moft con-
temptible, and moft worthlefs man in
his dominions, and to place him at the
head of the treafury the next week.
Thus far his majefty's prerogative un-
doubtedly extends; and the only fecu-
rity againft fuch an exertion of it, ex-
cepting the royal wifdom, is, that no
perfons of rank or character would act
with fuch a man, and that it is not very
probable that the parliament would grant
fupplies to fuch a minifter with much
liberality. But the extent of the royal
prerogative in this cafe is not a difputed
point. Your lordfhip, therefore, could
have no intention to enlighten your au-
ditors when you introduced this topic;
but it might ferve to throw fome ob-
fcurity over the matter in debate; and
you knew it to be a fubject on which

the

the generality would not choofe, from
motives of delicacy or of policy, to ex-
prefs themfelves with much perfpicuity.
At all events, your declamation in fupport of the prerogative would certainly
recommend you in one place; and, if
it did not recommend you fo much to
your countrymen at large, or if it did
not well harmonize with your former
fpeeches againft the pernicious influence
of the crown; yet, if it contributed to
eftablifh you in the royal favour, and in
the treafury, the great objects of your
ambition might poffibly be attained.
However this might be, when it is confidered, that one great purpofe for which
the new miniftry was formed, was to re-
duce the enormous and pernicious influence of the crown, it muft be mani-
feft, that the manner in which your lordfhip obtained from his majefty the office
you poffefs, was a natural ground of

2   jealoufy

jealoufy and of diftruft to the reft of your colleagues. Your lordfhip has faid in parliament of " the fyftem of fecret advifers," that it is " a baleful and ac-curfed fyftem*." In this opinion, my lord, you have the concurrence of the wifeft and beft men in this country; and their ardent wifh is, that it may not be revived under your lordfhip:

It appears, that before the deceafe of the Marquis of Rockingham, your lord-fhip had differed fo much in opinion from other members of the cabinet, that Mr. Fox had expreffed the greateft un-willingnefs to act in concert with you, and had declared his intentions of re-figning. The principal point in conteft was, the acknowledgment of the inde-pendence of America. Your lordfhip

* Almon's Parliamentary Debates, vol. XV. p. 47.

declared,

declared, as a reafon for not acceding to this meafure, that the fun of Britain would be fet for ever, when that event should have taken place. This, my lord, was a very proper fubject of confideration for the government of this country fome years fince: but it is now much too late. Whatever degradation Great Britain may have fuftained by her feparation from America, the event has already taken place. America *is* independent. We may as well debate whether the city of Calais, or the province of Normandy, fhall now be confidered as part of the Britifh empire, as whether the United colonies of America are now to come under that defcription. The only point that can at prefent be debated is, whether the parliament of Great Britain fhall formally acknowledge that independence; whether they fhall acknowledge a fact notorious to all the world.

This

This acknowledgment appears neceſſary, to our obtaining peace; but is in no re-ſpect neceſſary to aſcertain the fact. Thoſe weak, arbitrary, and violent meaſures, which have been adopted during the courſe of the preſent reign againſt the colonies of America, have eſtabliſhed their independence beyond any poſſibi-lity of prevention. Of this your lord-ſhip has too much underſtanding not to be convinced; though you may affect a contrary opinion, from an idea that a compliance with royal prejudices is the beſt method of obtaining the royal fa-vour.

To ſuppoſe that the inhabitants of America, after the blood, and ſlaughter, and devaſtation, which have marked the progreſs of the royal arms in that coun-try; after they have ſuccefsfully reſiſted the moſt vigorous efforts, and the greateſt armaments,

armaments, that we have been able to employ againſt them; after they have captured two Britiſh generals, and two Britiſh armies; after the royal troops have been nearly driven from the continent; and after the independence of the United States has been acknowledged by ſome of the firſt powers in Europe; to ſuppoſe, that after all this the Americans will again acknowledge the authority of the king of Great Britain, and give up their independence, is one of the weakeſt and moſt abſurd imaginations that can enter into any human underſtanding. I cannot, therefore, conceive your lordſhip to be capable of it; or that you could advance ſuch a ſentiment for any other purpoſe, than that of promoting thoſe temporary views which were ſuggeſted by your ambition.

At a period big with public danger, and

and public calamity, the diffolution of a
political confederacy, whofe united efforts
might have faved the nation, cannot be
too much lamented. It was very natural for Mr. Fox, who will be allowed
even by his enemies to poffefs no ordinary
degree of penetration, to refufe to continue
in the adminiftration, if a man were placed
at the head of it, whofe principles he
had difcovered to be in oppofition to his
own, and hoftile to the interefts of the
nation. But thofe who have formed a
juft eftimate of the great and compre-
henfive talents of Mr. Fox, of his energetic eloquence, of his weight and influence in parliament, and of the rectitude of thofe principles which he avows,
and by which he appears to be actuated,
muft confider his removal from office as
a great national evil. That your efforts
in the caufe of the public, that your parliamentary exertions were in any degree

to

to be compared with thofe of Mr. Fox, will hardly be pretended by the moft partial of your lordfhip's friends. But there was an opennefs, a manlinefs in Mr. Fox's character, which rendered him no favourite in the clofet. He could not ftoop to the mean arts of flattery; he was no adept in courtly adulation. In thefe qualities your lordfhip had manifeftly and greatly the advantage.

THE avidity with which your lordfhip grafped at the firft office of power and of influence, regardlefs of the fentiments of your colleagues; the fedulous induftry with which you courted royal favour, and the zeal which you difplayed in fupport of royal prerogative, notwithftanding your recent declamations againft the pernicious and ruinous influence of the crown; the cool indifference with which you

you faw yourfelf deferted by men of the moft fplendid talents, and in whom the public had placed the greateft confidence; thefe were circumftances ftrikingly characteriftic of difpofitions, totally repugnant to thofe of genuine patriotifm. It might be fuppofed, that the refignation of Mr. Fox was too precipitate; but this meafure might arife from views of the moft laudable nature, untinctured by perfonal animofity, or by any interefted or ambitious motives. He might be induced to take this ftep from a full conviction, that a new fyftem of fecret influence was commencing, under the aufpices of your lordfhip, and that you were engaged in the fupport of meafures pernicious to the beft interefts of your country. His conduct might be the refult of virtue, and of a real and ardent attachment to the public welfare; but who can affign any other motives for

D   your

your eagernefs to gain poffeffion of the treafury, but thofe of felfifhnefs and of ambition ? We may alfo afk, whether any but a prerogative minifter, whether any but a minifter who thought to maintain his ground by flattering the prince, would dare to threaten the council, or the parliament, with a revival, or exertion of the royal negative ? When a conduct like this is adopted by a minifter, juft brought into power upon great and public principles, and who had diftinguifhed himfelf by loud complaints againft the influence of the crown, is there not the utmoft reafon for fufpicion and diftruft, and for apprehending a treacherous defertion of the great interefts of the people ?

It has been one of the misfortunes attendant on your lordfhip, that your intrigues have been the means of lowering

ing the general opinion of two gentlemen, of whom the public have for fome years thought very highly. Your friendfhip may have contributed to enrich them, but it has been with fome diminution of character. I refer to the penfions which you procured for colonel Barrè and lord Afhburton; and of which you endeavoured to make the marquis of Rockingham appear the author. But notwithftanding your lordfhip's dexterity, the public have been undeceived upon that fubject. As to colonel Barrè, I acknowledge the merit and parliamentary fervices of that gentleman; but no man can reafonably expect to retain the character of a difinterefted patriot, if he eagerly embraces the firft opportunity of being repaid all that he has loft by that public fpirit, by which he might formerly be diftinguifhed. The colonel was put into poffeffion of a lucrative

D 2   place;

place; and should therefore have been content without a pension, though his place might not render him quite so rich, as he might have been if he had always voted as former ministers would have directed him. The acquisition of great wealth, and of a high reputation for patriotism, are not often to be expected by the same man. He who is solicitous to obtain the former, must generally be content to relinquish the latter. As to Mr. DUNNING, it required neither Grecian, nor Roman virtue, in a man who had accumulated so large a fortune by his profession, to promote the interests of his country without a pension. If the dignity of the peerage could not be supported without a pension, that acuteness of understanding by which Mr. Dunning has always been distinguished, should have taught him, that the title of Lord Ashburton, when accompanied with a penfion,

penfion, would not be an acceffion of dignity, but a real degradation. But this is a fubject on which I am not difpofed to dwell; the merits of Mr. Dunning as a conftitutional lawyer, and his important parliamentary fervices, have defervedly raifed him high in the eftimation of his country; and I am forry that their luftre fhould in any degree have been tarnifhed, by his defcent into a peerage.

The concurrence in thefe penfions, and the defence of them, appear to me to be the moft cenfurable part of the conduct of Mr. Fox and of Mr. Burke, during the fhort time that they were in adminiftration. It was probably a facrifice that was made to peace, and to your lordfhip; but it was a facrifice that ought not to have been made. They fhould have had the firmnefs to refift

every

every meafure of this kind, and not have
been led to countenance any thing of fo
exceptionable a nature, either by complai-
fance to your lordfhip, and your friends,
or by any perfonal efteem for the gentlemen on whom the penfions were conferred. A miniftry brought in on great
and public principles, fhould have ad-
hered to thofe principles; and not have
hazarded their credit with the nation,
by conferring penfions even on the moft
meritorious of their friends. It was of
infinite importance to maintain their reputation with the people; and this could
hardly be done, by giving penfions to
fome of their own party, almoft as foon
as they came into office. The gentlemen on whom thefe penfions were conferred were, indeed, the more immediate
friends of your lordfhip; but the whole
of the new adminiftration naturally in-
curred fome part of the public cenfure

5   on

on the occafion. If there were any honourable method by which penfions
might have been conferred on Mr. Barrè
and Mr. Dunning, as a reward for their
public fervices, the merit of which I am
in no refpect inclined to leffen, it muft
have been by a vote of parliament, in a
manner fimilar to that lately beftowed
on Mr. Grattan by the parliament of Ire-
land. But grants of this kind by minifters only, and by minifters whofe eloquence againft penfions was fo ftrongly
in every man's memory, and to gentlemen who had themfelves difplayed equal
eloquence on the fame fubject, were not
likely to increafe the public confidence in
the new adminiftration, or to convince
mankind that their principles and conduct were perfectly fuitable to their pro-
feffions.

ONE circumftance which has contributed

buted to prevent the nation from wholly
defpairing, that fome meafures might be
adopted beneficial to the kingdom, though
your lordfhip prefides in the adminiftration, is, that fuch men as the Duke of
Richmond, Lord Camden, and Lord
Keppel, ftill remain in office. It cannot,
indeed, be expected, that thefe noblemen
will continue to act in concert with
you, if they fee you openly promoting
meafures ruinous to the nation. But
they may continue in office, till they dif-
cover it abfolutely neceffary to quit all
connexion with you, and then find too
late, that they have contributed to the
promotion of your defigns, and to the
eftablifhment of your power; and that
they have unintentionally been the means
of injuring their country. As to the
DUKE OF RICHMOND, the general tenor
of his conduct in parliament has given
him a juft claim to public confidence

and

applaufe. He has laboured with great
zeal, with great ability, and with inde-
fatigable induftry, to promote the national interefts ; free from ariftocratic
prejudices, he has nobly fupported the
rights of the people at large ; and has
exerted himfelf, in a manner that muft
ever be remembered to his honour, to
procure a more juft and equal parliamentary reprefentation.

WHEN Mr. Fox retired from adminiftration, your lordfhip was naturally
apprehenfive of a powerful oppofition
in parliament ; and you difcovered no
ordinary fhare of fkill in political ma-
nœuvres, when you prevailed on Mr.
WILLIAM PITT to take a part in the
new miniftry, as now formed; by which
he might be induced to enter the lifts
with Mr. Fox, and thereby afford your
lordfhip fome affiftance and fupport

E   againft

against the vigorous attacks of that very formidable orator. It can, indeed, be no wonder, that so young a man as Mr. Pitt, however splendid his talents, should have been brought over to enlist under the banners of your lordship. Admitting him to be actuated by the purest motives, he could not be supposed to be a match for that art and dexterity, of which you are known to be so great a master. Whatever your intentions might be, you doubtless gave them the most plausible appearance: and it must be flattering to young ambition, to be called to fill so important an office in the state, as that which he now holds at so early a period of life. The time may possibly arrive, when he will not consider his connexion with your lordship as a fortunate circumstance for his reputation: but, at all events, I hope that his future conduct will not disgrace his talents

lents and his defcent. Should he find,
that he is brought into power only to
promote the ambitious defigns of others,
and to fupport that SECRET INFLUENCE
of which his noble father fo pathetically
complained, that fecret influence which
has made fuch rapid ftrides towards the
deftruction of this country; whenever he
fhall have made this difcovery, it may reafonably be hoped, that he will inftanta-
neoufly quit fuch connexions, which
muft be fo dangerous to his honour and
his fame, and adopt fuch a line of conduct as will be worthy of the fon of the
illuftrious CHATHAM: In one meafure,
of great national importance, he has already pledged himfelf to the public; and
cannot defert the interefts of the people
without a total forfeiture of his reputation. I will not, therefore, fuppofe this
poffible; but fhall prefume that we may
reft affured, that a bill for a more equal

reprefentation

reprefentation of the people will receive
from Mr. PITT the moft unequivocal,
firm, and vigorous fupport.

THE prefent parliamentary reprefentation of this country is fo extremely partial and inadequate, that it requires an
immediate and fubftantial reform ; and
no object can be more worthy of the attention of the people at large, nor is
there any which they ought more ar-
dently and fteadily to labour to attain,
than a more equal reprefentation. The
difficulties, which are fometimes urged
refpecting this great bufinefs, have in
them much more of imagination, than
of reality. They are either ftarted by
the timid and the indolent, or by artful
men who diflike the meafure, but who
have too ftrong a conviction of its rectitude, to venture to oppofe it openly and
explicitly. If your lordfhip fhould fin-
cerely

cerely employ the influence you have obtained with his majefty, in the promotion of this great and important national object, it will contribute, beyond any thing elfe, to reftore you to the confidence of your country.

As the removal of Mr. Fox from office is a public evil, in the fame light muft be confidered the lofs of Mr. EDMUND BURKE. That gentleman poffeffes fuch a fplendour of genius, he has difplayed fuch an extent of knowledge, and fuch uncommon powers of eloquence, as have long excited the general admiration. Nor is he entitled to lefs efteem for the qualities of his heart, than for thofe of his underftanding. It is, however, to be regretted, that this amiable man, this elegant and claffic orator, fhould not be more a friend to fhortening the duration of parliament, and equalizing the reprefentation

ſentation of the people, than he has been generally ſuppoſed. He ſeems too much under the influence of ariſtocratic prejudices, though the uniform integrity of his conduct entitles him to our fulleſt confidence in the rectitude of his intentions. Whatever may be his defects, they are ſo much over-balanced by his merits, that his removal from power is greatly to be lamented; and if public ſervices, hitherto unrewarded, are to be recompenſed by penſions, no man can have a better claim than Mr. Burke. When colonel Barrè took poſſeſſion of the office of paymaſter of the forces, it is natural to ſuppoſe, that he muſt feel ſomewhat aukward at the recollection, that the late paymaſter had neither place nor penſion.

BUT if Mr. Fox and Mr. BURKE have ceaſed to form any part of the adminiſtration

ftration of this country, your lordfhip
has procured a very induftrious and diftinguifhed affociate in the LORD-ADVO-
CATE OF SCOTLAND. Great as the in-
feriority of his talents may be to theirs,
he is fuperior to either of them in tracta-
bility. Your lordfhip cares lefs about
men, than about meafures; and he will
be as indifferent about meafures as your
lordfhip can be about men. You may
acquire political philofophy from each
other; but it is hoped, that a regard to
your mutual intereft will not be forgot-
ten. We may at leaft anfwer for the
Lord Advocate, that he will not forget
his own. This being fecured, he will
not be inflexible in other points: and
it may be extremely ufeful to your lordfhip to have an affociate of fuch commo-
dious pliability,

—————————— *Qui femper, & omni*
Nocte dieque poteft alienum fumere vultum.

2   IT

IT is alfo one of the excellencies of this great lawyer, that he has not " weak " nerves * ;" and will not defert, for flight circumftances, any caufe in which his employers may think proper to engage him. Should the moft improvident and extravagant terms be agreed to for a public loan, he can maintain, as he did in behalf of lord North, in oppofition to Sir George Savile, that the minifter had not " made a corrupt bargain for any bad pur- " pofe, but had acted with all poffible in- " tegrity and induftry, and to the advan- " tage of the public †." He can prove, that ſt is juft, and reafonable, and proper, that a minifter fhould be partial to his friends in the diftribution of a public loan. " A minifter muft be a mere lump of " ice, divefted of paffions, of friendſhip

---

* *Vid.* Almon's Parliamentary Regifter, vol. II. of the prefent Parliament, p. 346, 347.

† Ibid. p. 345.

" and

" and feeling, could he furmount this " kind of partiality *." Should any fteps be taken to leffen the public expenditure, or to regulate the expences of the crown, Mr. Dundas can maintain, that the civil lift revenue is " a pofitive freehold," and a " perfonal eftate;" and that we ought not " to lay violent hands upon " property the moft facred ;" or to " abo- " lifh places which had been created by " the wifdom of our forefathers +." He can affert, that a vote of parliament againft the influence of the crown would be " replete with danger to the con- " ftitution ‡." He can oppofe laying an account of penfions before parlia-

* *Vid.* Almon's Parliamentary Regifter, vol. II. of the prefent Parliament, p. 348.

+ Speech of the Lord-advocate on the fecond reading of Mr. Burke's bill, Parliam. Reg. p. 48.

‡ Lord-advocate's fpeech in oppofition to Mr. Dunning's motion, Parliam. Reg. vol. XVII. p. 466.

F   ment‑

ment * : and fhould any propofals be
made for an inquiry into naval tranfactions, he can prove, that this is very
unfit and improper ; becaufe there are
" many incidents and circumftances in
" the navy, which the Houfe of Com-
" mons ought not to inquire into †."
He can alfo harangue upon the dangers
that attend public meetings of the
people ; and can call upon parliament to
fupprefs county affociations §.

It was obferved by lord Maitland, in
the houfe of commons, in the debate on
the petition from the county-delegates,
that the doctrines laid down by the lord-
advocate, in his fpeech in oppofition to

* *Vid.* his fpeech in oppofition to Sir Geo. Savile's motion
for laying the lift of penfions before parliament,
Parliam. Reg. vol. XVII. p. 137.

† Speech of the Lord-advocate, Feb. 19, 1781. Parliam.
Reg. vol. XVIII. p. 511.

§ Ibid. p. 283.

the

the reception of that petition, were fuch,
as, he trufted, " would never be fuffered
" to pafs without indignation or con-
" tempt. They were hoftile to the
" foundations of Britifh freedom, and as
" contrary to law as they were to the
" conftitution *." Yet this man your
lordfhip has felected, as one of the defenders of your meafures, and his ad-
miffion into office is one of the firft fruits
of your adminiftration. You have been
the means of depriving the nation of the
fervices of Mr. Fox and Mr. Burke ; but
you have made ample recompence by
the introduction into power of HENRY
DUNDAS.

MR. Fox has fometimes drawn the
character of your new affociate in pretty
ftrong colours. In one of his fpeeches,

---

* Speech of the Lord-advocate, Feb. 19, 1781. Parliam.
Reg. vol. XVIII. p. 241.

he

he faid of him, that he was one of thofe men " whofe inflammatory harangues " had led the nation, ftep by ftep, from " violence to violence, in that inhuman " unfeeling fyftem of blood and maffacre, " which every honeft man muft deteft, " which every good man muft abhor, " and every wife man condemn +." In truth, my lord, your bringing this gentleman into office, fo foon after your elevation to the treafury, and the avowal which that appointment implied of your want of fuch a defender, and fuch an af-fiftant, or of your being under fome fecret influence not favourable to the interefts of your country, afford an evidence of your own principles not very equivocal. No honeft minifter could have any occafion for fuch an advocate. If it were neceffary for the fake of national impar-

+ Parliam. Reg. vol. XVI. p. 123.

tiality,

tiality, that fome natives of Scotland fhould be brought into office, on the formation of a new adminiftration, fuch men as lord Stair, or lord Maitland, ought to have been introduced, men who had evinced fome attachment to the common interefts of the country, and not one of the moft zealous and active defenders of the worft meafures of the laft miniftry.

However your lordfhip may flatter yourfelf on the addrefs and dexterity which have characterized your political intrigues, it is not probable that they will be finally fuccefsful. It is not eafy, my Lord, for the moft artful man to deceive long. It may be infinuated by your friends, and favourites, and flatterers, that Mr. Fox's refignation, becaufe he would not act in concert with you, originated in ambition. But no fophiftry

can

can make it even plaufible, that your
conduct was the refult of patriotifm. It
might be neceffary for Mr. Fox to refign,
in order to give a fignal to the nation,
that the old fyftem was reviving. But
no motives of a public nature could
have induced your lordfhip to divide the
cabinet, that you might obtain the firft
feat at the board of treafury. If Mr.
Fox found, that the principles upon
which you acted in the cabinet, whilft
fecretary of ftate, were fo inconfiftent
with the real interefts of the nation, as
to induce him repeatedly to declare his
intentions of refigning, his unwillingnefs
to continue in adminiftration with you
muft be naturally increafed, when he faw
you placed at the head of the treafury,
by which you would neceffarily gain a
great acceffion of weight and of influence; and by which you might be ena-
bled to defeat thofe meafures, which he

5   confidered

confidered as effential to the falvation of the nation. I am far from fuppofing Mr. Fox to be deftitute of ambition; he makes no fuch pretenfions; but I hope, that his ambition is perfectly confiftent with the welfare of his country; and that he has a juft fenfe of the value of that fame which he has already obtained, and of that affection and regard with which he is viewed by his countrymen; for the lofs of which, nothing in the power of kings to beftow can be a compenfation.

You, my Lord, had an opportunity of acquiring that fair fame which is the reward of virtue, and which vice, however decorated by titles or by ribbands, never can obtain. That opportunity, I fear, you have loft for ever. You may have gained the favour of the King; but you have made an ill bargain,

gain, if you have purchaſed it by deſerting the cauſe of your country; and by the ſacrifice of your honour, and your conſcience. If your lordſhip has become the prime inſtrument in the revival and ſupport of that SECRET INFLUENCE, to which this country owes ſo many of its calamities, it is not eaſy to ſtate a greater degree of moral or political criminality.

BUT I leave you, my Lord, to your own reflections. Your own heart will beſt inform you, whether you have been influenced by any principles of virtue, or of public ſpirit, or merely by motives of private intereſt or ambition. If you have been actuated only by the latter, if you have abandoned the cauſe of the public, if you have ſacrificed the welfare of your country, to obtain a greater portion of royal favour,

no

no fituation can confer dignity upon
you. You may be flattered by the vain,
the venal, and the interefted; but you
will for ever forfeit the efteem and regard
of men of virtue, of the friends of freedom and their country; you will be ex-
ecrated by the prefent age, and by pofte-
rity.

I am,

My Lord,

Your Lordfhip's, &c;

F I N I S.